SCREAM BABY SCREAM

SONIA PALERMO

PLAYLIST

"Scream"—Avenged Sevenfold
"liMOusIne"—Bring Me The Horizon, AURORA
"Send the Pain Below"—Chevelle
"E-GIRLS ARE RUINING MY LIFE!"—CORPSE,
Savage Ga$p
"Passenger"—Deftones
"Risk"—Deftones
"Hunting Season"—Ice Nine Kills
"Sinner"—Of Virtue
"Sugar"—Sleep Token
"Granite"—Sleep Token
"Hypnosis"—Sleep Token
"Jaws"—Sleep Token
"Psycho Killer"—The Talking Heads
"Obsession"—Thornhill
"BEG!"—Vana

A Note From The Author

Scream Baby Scream is a dark, MFM Halloween Romance. Some content within this novella may be disturbing or triggering for some readers. Reader discretion is advised. Your mental health is a priority.

Subjects include alcohol use, drugging, knife play, choking/breath play, self-harm (cutting, off-page), marking (cutting, on-page), graphic sexual scenes, sadomasochism, and strong language. Any character depicted in a sexual scene is at least 18 years of age. This book should not be used as a reference or guide for safe BDSM practices.

Kinks, tropes, and fetishes include strangers-to-lovers, free use, masked men, stretching/DVP, choking/breath play, secret identity, mute MMC, dirty talking MMC, alt FMC, tattoos and piercings, voyeurism, knife play, multiple O's, praise, filming, marking (cutting, on-page), blood play, drugging, autassassinophilia (arousal by risk of being killed), sadomasochism, dubious consent, and consensual non-consent.

This is an MFM romance with a HEA guaranteed.

DEDICATION

To all the good girls who dream of getting railed by Ghostface. Why settle for one when you can have two?

"Let the impulse to love and the instinct to kill entangle to one."

—*Vessel, Sleep Token*

1

I look like a slut-shamer's wet dream.

It's the vibe I'm going for, but I prefer to avoid lingering, roving stares from creepy men twice my age unless I want to fuck them. And I don't want to fuck my tactless Uber driver.

He must be pushing sixty, which isn't usually a problem; Jeffrey Dean Morgan would totally get it if he weren't married and if I had a chance in hell. But it would be a major inconvenience if I gave this dude a heart attack—until I get to The Mansion, at least.

Twenty painfully slow minutes of uncomfortable small talk crawl by, and by the time we're balls deep in the Surrey Hills approaching the Cambrook Private Estate, I'm ready to end it all. Cause of death: eternal boredom.

The Prius pulls up to a pair of wrought-iron gates. I exit the car carefully, making sure the creeper doesn't catch a glimpse of my ass as I leave. I quickly rearrange my costume, fix my hair, then press the buzzer.

A woman's voice crackles through the speakers. "Password?"

I clear my throat and roll my eyes, recognising Daisy, my best friend's PA. "Titsoak."

Did I mention Cara is hilarious? Sometimes I wonder how I ended up friends with someone who supports narcissistic vampires and creepy werewolves, but then I remember she's pretty fucking awesome and the reason for this epic party.

"Tatum? Where the hell have you been, loca?" Daisy chimes in. She has an equally disturbing obsession with *The Twilight Saga*. Not that I'm one to judge—I have my own tastes that will never see the light of day.

Before I have time to respond, she buzzes me in. The heavy gates wind open, and I make my way up the long gravel path, lit only by flickering pumpkin lanterns in the otherwise pitch-black surroundings.

The wind picks up, whipping around me and stroking the flesh beneath my barely-there skirt, making me shiver. Music blasts through the house as I enter, the slow, driving rhythm of *Deftones'* "Passenger" amplifying the brooding atmosphere. It feels like I've stepped straight into a teen slasher movie.

The place is decked out with skeletons, bats, and cobwebs. Dense fog swirls around my chunky black boots in the dim red light, while the air is thick with the mingling scents of expensive perfume and top-shelf alcohol.

Small groups lounge on the steps of an ornate mahogany staircase, and the steady flow of bodies sipping from plastic cups and puffing berry-scented vapes makes it hard to spot Cara, Daisy, or anyone else I might know.

Nineties final girls seem to be a recurring theme; women in low-slung jeans and tight white tank tops splayed with fake blood, some in grey space overalls reminiscent of the *Alien* franchise. And judging by all the slasher masks, spicy booktok is no longer a well-kept secret, either.

The unease of seeing so many hidden faces settles in, but my body betrays me as a rush of warmth spreads between my legs. I squeeze my thighs just as a pair of hands grab my bare ass, nearly making me jump out of my skin. I spin around quickly, ready to confront whoever dared to touch me, only to hear a familiar giggle.

Relief washes over me, and my warning glare softens. "Bro, I was about to snap your arm, I swear..." I trail off, my attention snagged by Cara's costume. She's dressed as Dani from *Midsommar*, complete with a huge floral headdress that cascades down her lingerie-clad body, adorned with vibrant blooms. It must have taken her hours to put together.

"Any excuse to fuck a bitch up," she says with a grin, striking a pose. "That outfit is fire, by the way."

My obvious choice would have been Maxine Minx, given my dark hair and freckles, and my love for Mia Goth. Unfortunately, I can't quite pull off dungarees and side boob like she does. Instead, I went for an all-black ensemble, complete with a corset, tulle skirt, and mismatched stockings. "Thank you, boo. Likewise."

Cara smiles proudly. "Daisy helped me. She's a keeper."

For a moment, an expression of fleeting self-consciousness crosses Cara's face, as if she's just realised she might have overshared. It stings a bit; she should know by now that I'm not the type to judge. She clears her throat and changes the subject. "Anyway, what are you drinking?"

"Anything, as long as it's neat," I reply. The quicker I calm my nerves, the better.

"Tequila?"

"Perfect." She turns on her heel and disappears around the corner, leaving me to savour the atmosphere—alive and electric with chatter, swaying hips, and bursts of laughter.

I can't help but envy the incredible makeup and costumes around me, but painting my face would have been pointless. By the end of the night, it'll be streaked with tears and who knows what else.

In the midst of my musings, my phone vibrates with a text, pulling me out of my thoughts.

Unknown: You look pretty...

Butterflies swarm in my stomach, their frantic flapping screaming danger as bubbles appear on the screen. I try to reassure myself, reminding myself that it's just a game, but the intensity of it all feels strikingly real.

Unknown: ... for a dead girl.

My gaze flits nervously around the room, darting from one person to another. My heart skips beats as a wave of panic and arousal washes over me, the ache between my legs intensifying. I realise with growing discomfort that everyone around me is deeply engaged in conversation, their phones nowhere in sight.

Clever bastard.

Another vibration from my phone jolts me again just as Cara and a very cute-looking Daisy return with six plastic shot glasses balanced between them. The tiny blonde is dressed in a bear costume, and it takes me a minute to realise that they've come as a pair. I'd always had an inkling that there was more to these two, but it's really none of my business. Their mutual happiness is all I care about.

When I finally have the chance to look at my screen without seeming rude, my excitement dampens. It's just a notification from a dating app I've been using—and gotten nowhere with—for a while. I ignore it and slide it into my thigh-highs before taking a shot glass from each of them. If tonight doesn't go my way, I'll be cancelling my subscription.

"Dude, you're a fucking genius," I say, addressing Daisy. "You should be a wardrobe stylist, not this bitch's assistant."

"That's what I keep saying," Cara says, smiling. "I'm keeping her for my own selfish reasons."

"And I'm staying for mine," Daisy counters.

Fuck, the cuteness of these two is super sweet and nauseating in equal measure.

"Seriously, your costumes are amazing." I hold up both shot glasses. "Cheers to another successful movie."

The distinct taste of butterscotch and caramel glides over my tongue as I knock back one shot, then the next. The burn at the base of my throat is a little less intense with the second shot, accompanied by the satisfying aftertaste of sweetness and spice that instantly relaxes my body and calms my nerves.

My phone vibrates against my leg. I stack the plastic glasses and retrieve the device from my hold-up.

Unknown: I want to play a game.

A sheet of goosebumps scatters up my spine, my neck tingling with the sensation at being watched. Glancing around the room, I try and fail to pinpoint the perpetrator as the playlist switches to something a little less serious, the funky intro offsetting the dark subject matter of the *Talking Heads'* classic "Psycho Killer." I'm grateful to be third-wheeling this conversation so I can subtly focus on finding this mystery person.

When I look up, fear grips my stomach.

Dressed in black jeans and a black hoodie, a white, ghost-like mask stares straight at me from the wooden balustrade. Even though I can't see their face, I can feel the weight of their stare beneath those dark, stretched-out eye sockets, and it's all on me.

Suddenly, the music cuts out, replaced in an instant by the iconic '80s banger from *The Breakfast Club*. The abrupt shift is jarring, a stark contrast to the macabre playlist. The cheerful intro is a welcome distraction, but it makes me wonder why the DJ has strayed from the spooky theme.

As *Simple Minds* plays out, the masked stranger raises a gloved finger to their mouth in a shushing motion. Before I have a chance to react, all eyes turn to me, accompanied by laughter and clapping. In reality, they're gawking at what's behind me. Reluctantly, I turn around to see a group dressed as The Brat Pack. The gang's all there—the nerd, the jock, the princess, the basket case, and the criminal.

The person dressed as Judd Nelson's character has already done two fist pumps in five seconds, and I can tell that's going to get old fast. I turn back toward my conversation, looking up, hoping the person I was watching is still there. But all I see is a group of strangers.

Right then, my phone vibrates again.

Unknown: Do you want to die tonight?

2

"I'll be right back," I say, excusing myself, butterflies erupting in my stomach as an invisible force draws me towards the stairs. As I ascend, each step feels heavier with anticipation. It's risky business, this game I'm playing, but I chose it for myself.

How did I get here? Months of constant messaging with a stranger I met through ConsciousKink have led me to this moment. Wes knows my deepest desires—every thought, every fantasy, every depravity laid out for him to decode and accept.

Like the one where I play the helpless victim to a masked killer at a Halloween party.

Most men are all talk; I never thought we'd actually get to meet. Yet here we are.

The top floor is shrouded in darkness, illuminated only by a large bay window. I veto the option to explore, heading right, toward a softly lit room at the end of the corridor.

Horror movie 101 tells me to ignore it. Logic tells me to run the other way and never look back. But I thrive on fear. I love the rush of adrenaline I get when I'm scared, so much that if Wes and I hadn't already established a safeword and discussed limits, I'm still unsure if I'd run the other way.

Challenge accepted.

Tentatively, I walk through the hallway, my obnoxiously loud boots echoing on the hardwood floors. I need to be stealthy about this, even though something tells me it's pointless, that I'm already falling right into his trap.

He wants this. But I want this, too. I *chose* this.

With each dark door I pass, I glance behind me, making sure there's nobody following me. Finally, I reach the third and final room at the end of the corridor. It's slightly ajar, and I'm almost certain that he's in there. I take a deep breath, bracing myself for what's on the other side, and push it open.

Citrus and herbs, earth, and wood. It smells like a forest. A four-poster bed stands in the centre, with its walnut wood headboard propped against inky-blue panelling that's decorated with hanging plants dying of thirst and rustic paintings of gothic houses and eerie landscapes.

Candles in varying proportions are propped up on antique candlesticks, spread between the bedside table, the unused fireplace, and a small wooden console table beside a sash window. A thin trail of smoke rises from a stick of incense.

I click the door closed and assess my surroundings. He can't be far if he's the one doing something as reckless as leaving lit candles and incense unattended. Still, I can't help but think it's pretty and cosy. The luxury burgundy bedding and matching throw make it… romantic and inviting. Definitely a fucking trap.

My heart is racing as I bend to search under the bed, but it's unlikely that anyone could hide underneath; it's far too close to the floor.

Being named after one of the most iconic horror characters of all time means it's within my birthright to be a total horror whore, but this is still scaring the ever-loving shit out of me.

Steam rolls through the cracked-open door of the en-suite as I cautiously approach, bracing myself for the jump scare of my life.

Why do I do this to myself?

It seemed like such a great idea at the time, to proposition a stranger to come and fulfil my depraved fantasy, I just never expected the suspense to be this good.

Don't get your hopes up, Tatum. Put on your big girl pants and go into that room before the party's over.

My heart gallops in anticipation as I walk toward the door, my pussy throbbing with desire, aching to be touched. Part of me wants him to show up and end this creepy game of house, while another part craves the full experience—to be pushed to my limit, my body dripping with anticipation, to embrace the fear before the final reveal.

"Fuck it," I say out loud and push the door open.

Shower steam clogs the air, the sharp scent of menthol and camphor filling my lungs. Navigating through the haze, I reach out for something to steady myself. Finally, I find the huge glass shower enclosure. I turn off the water and lean against the cool, green tiles, waiting for the steam to clear.

There's nobody else here.

I should be telling myself, a twenty-eight-year-old capable and self-assured woman, to get a grip. But he's playing me masterfully, and I'm falling prey to his game.

I go to leave, but something in the mirror above the basin catches my eye.

"Trick or Treat."

This could mean one of two things—it's part of the party décor, or Wes has been here.

I snap a selfie in the mirror and send it to *Unknown*, captioning it, "Is that the best you can do?"

I'm excited to see where this is headed, but I'm also hyperaware that he could show up unannounced at any moment. The possibility that he could be anywhere, ready to pounce, sends a rush of adrenaline through my bloodstream.

Curiosity draws me back into the bedroom, where everything remains untouched. Candles and incense burn steadily, filling the air with a heady mix reminiscent of the woods, conjuring memories of the boy who took my virginity on a forest floor. The distinct scent stirs something in me—comfort and nostalgia for simpler times, when all my rage was channeled into the razor I used to grip in the bathtub. Now, tattoos cover the scars, the ink serving as a constant reminder of what lies beneath.

I shake my head to dispel my thoughts. I shouldn't be getting sidetracked when a hot-as-hell masked man is on the loose.

I grab a candleholder from the fireplace and blow out the flame, discarding the wax pillar and gripping the long brass curves. It's heavy in my hand, and I doubt I'll need it, but it might be useful to have a weapon. Plus, it makes me feel like a badass.

Creeping over to the door that separates me and whatever the hell is lurking in the shadows, I venture back into the hallway, staying quiet and vigilant as I pass the first door without a hitch. As I approach the second door, a creak echoes behind me.

Fuck.

My heart plummets and then pounds, relentlessly threatening to burst through my ribcage. I slowly turn around, bracing myself to face my stalker. But there's nobody there.

I hold my breath and turn again, only to see a figure in a white mask with fabric-covered, curved black holes for eyes and a gaping, blacked-out mouth reminiscent of Edvard Munch's infamous painting, staring at me from ten feet away.

"Is that supposed to intimidate me?" I ask, trying to sound defiant, though my voice trembles.

He slowly tilts his head sideways—a classic serial killer move that sends my pulse into overdrive and sparks heat between my legs.

Suddenly, he lunges toward me. Fueled by adrenaline, I turn and sprint down the hallway. But just as I approach the first door, it swings open, catching me off guard and revealing another figure in a ghostly mask. A jolt of terror surges through me, paralysing my thoughts. I don't have time to process that there are two of them, so I keep running to the end of the corridor, but—

Within seconds, a gloved hand grips my arm, dragging me backward. His arousal presses against my spine as he locks me in his grasp—one arm across my chest, the other hand clamped over my mouth. The dizzying scent of leather and smoke overwhelms me. My body betrays me, igniting a primal need that makes me crave him even as my mind screams for escape.

3

"Remember your safeword?" he rasps, his voice deep and deliciously dark. I'm certain this is Wes. This *must* be Wes. I attempt a nod, though his hold on me makes it hard. "Good girl."

But what if it isn't? It's the first time I've heard his voice, and I can only imagine how he sounds talking dirty to me after months of digital foreplay. He's much taller and broader than I initially thought; he could probably kill me without even trying. I clench my thighs at the thought. I shouldn't be this turned on after being blindsided, yet here we are. We've all concluded that fear gets me off.

I'm desperate to turn around, but my thoughts turn to mush when he loosens his grip, his gloved hand sliding off my mouth and down to the apex of my thighs. A pathetic whimper escapes my throat when the leather makes contact with the thin lace fabric of my thong.

"Shh…" he purrs, sending a sheet of goosebumps across my spine. "Don't scream, dead girl. Be a good little victim for me." He pushes my thong aside, and my legs buckle as he slides a finger along my slit. "Fuck, baby. You're soaked."

I suck in a breath as my eyes roll back. His fingers feel so good that I almost forget about the unexpected guest.

"Who was that?" I manage to utter, breathy and strained.

"Who? It's just us, baby."

Baby.

He says it with such conviction that I almost believe him. But this is just two people meeting for the first time after months of online flirting, meant for a single night of play. If he truly believes it's just us here, then either I'm hallucinating or someone is watching us.

"No, there was another…" The words die on my tongue when he plunges two fingers inside me, my mouth gaping at the intrusion, my breath violently leaving my lungs. "Oh, fuck."

I press my hips against his rigid cock, my pussy throbbing as his fingertips stretch apart inside me.

"Eager little slut, aren't you?" he hums. "Does it make you wet knowing how hard I am for you?" The feel of his arousal digging into my back makes me weak, almost tipping me over the edge. His words weaken my resolve, chipping away at my defences as I feel myself surrendering completely. It's embarrassing how close I am to coming already.

As if he can read my thoughts, he withdraws, leaving me reeling from the sudden loss, and holds his hand in front of my face. Glistening strings spread between his fingers as he scissors them apart. Then, without warning, he shoves them into my mouth, his thick fingers gliding over my taste buds as I suck my arousal from the soft leather. The earthy, almost sweet flavors mix as I swirl my tongue around them.

He hums, pushing them deeper into my throat. "Such a good girl for me. How about you show me what else that pretty mouth can do?" He snatches the candlestick from my hand. "Or perhaps you want me to fuck you with this?"

I have no comeback, not when my mouth is full of leather and spit and my own juices. I'm still reeling from his fingers being inside me, and the total mindfuck of the other masked person. But mostly because he's right, I'm desperate to be filled, and the thought of him fucking me with an antique candlestick makes my pussy ache with need.

Loosening his grip, he withdraws his fingers and guides me into the second bedroom, a smaller, brighter version of the other, alight with candles.

"On your knees, baby," he says, pointing to a deep green ottoman by the window. "Over there."

I kneel with my hands splayed on the windowsill, peering out into the quiet darkness below. It's eerie, like the tense calm before a jump scare in a movie. The only sound is the faint thrum of bass reverberating through the floorboards. As I glance up, Wes's masked reflection looms behind me, dark and dominant.

"You're so fucking perfect, you know that?" he says, his torturous voice making my pussy ache. "Let's fix that. I want to make a mess of you. Keep watching that window, baby."

Bending to his knees behind me, he dips his head between my legs. His warm breath fans my pussy, making me shiver as his tongue sweeps along my slit.

"Oh, my god," I rasp, already struggling for air as I dig my nails into the wood.

"God ain't here, baby. Just your friendly neighbourhood serial killer." Something cold and hard glides across my skin, hooking under the fabric of my thong. My body tenses at the familiar feel of a blade against my flesh, the thought of him slicing my skin both exciting and terrifying. He fists my underwear in the dip above my ass and snaps it off. "Much better." I imagine him tilting his head to admire his handiwork, but the sharp smack of his palm against my pussy jolts me back to reality, making me gasp. "Tonight, this cunt belongs to me, to use as I please." *Smack*. I suck in a breath, revelling in the sting. "And it's too damn pretty, too damn *mine,* to hide. By the time I'm through with you, you'll be questioning everything."

I brace myself against the windowsill, my hips pushed back as Wes presses down on me. I spread my knees wider, feeling his head dip between my legs. I throw my head back, closing my eyes and arching my back in desperation as he laps at my slit—hard, firm, and almost cruel—before he sucks my clit between his teeth, eliciting a wild, almost feral moan from deep within.

"Mm, so wet for me," he says, holding something cold, hard, and sharp at my entrance. "Keep still. Unless you want me to slice right through your perfect little cunt."

My first instinct is to turn around and snatch the knife from his grasp, but I'm frozen, scared to move or even breathe in case he cuts me. A ridiculous thought, given my history.

"Just relax," he coos. "I could wreck this delicate, perfect pussy so damn easily. Imagine my knife going deeper and deeper. Imagine how good it would feel to fuck the cold, hard steel as it slices through your insides, killing you in a slow, achingly beautiful kind of way."

My breathing escalates, a confusing mix of fear and arousal.

He presses the knife against my skin, the cold edge sending a shiver through me. Slowly, he nudges the blade deeper, the pressure increasing until I feel the sharpness threatening to slice my skin. Each inch feels deliberate, a tantalising dance between pain and pleasure. I can't help but clench around it, my body responding to the gradual intrusion.

"Need to call red?" he asks, his voice low and probing.

I swallow, the mix of fear and arousal making my voice tremble. "No."

I may be completely unhinged for allowing someone to violate me like this, but I've had worse things inside my pussy. Like those toxic devil dicks that show up at 3 a.m., an extension of low-frequency douchebags who quote *The Alchemist* and expect women to flock to them because they're so *spiritual*.

"That's my good girl. Deep breaths, baby."

Weirdly, I trust Wes. Even as the knife presses deeper, I squeeze my eyes shut, focusing on the scratching of the blade as it penetrates gradually, my walls clenching tighter around it with each inch. He goes slowly, and I count each breath.

"You think I don't see your darkness in those pretty scars?" he murmurs, easing the blade deeper. "You're a haunted house, Tatum. So perfectly cursed. I could fuck you senseless with this knife until you're screaming in pain and pleasure, your insides torn apart as you beg for me to stop. But I won't stop, baby. I'd fuck you like a savage. Ruthless. Unapologetic. I'd violate you 'til your insides are dripping down my cock, until your swollen little pussy has us soaked in blood and cum, pleasure and pain and your sweet fucking juices."

Just when I think he's about to relent, he pushes the blade in deeper, eliciting a sharp gasp as I brace myself, ready to call my safeword. But then he pulls back, slowly retracting the knife while his fingers spread me open.

Wes stands behind me, the knife raised, its tip glinting in the moonlight. He tilts his mask just enough to expose his mouth and sticks out his long, flat tongue, dragging it from base to tip along the edge of the knife. "Mm. Your fear tastes exquisite."

He trails the blade along my throat, pressing it gently against my chin to coax it upward. Wes threads his fingers through my hair, gripping my scalp firmly as he tugs the strands, forcing my head back to expose my neck.

I study the contours of his lower face: the dark, rugged stubble on a sharp jawline, and his full, puffy lips glistening with my juices. This fleeting glimpse is both mesmerising and unsettling. It's a stark reminder that the person towering over me is real, someone who knows me on a level deeper than anyone I've ever known. The realisation is as daunting as it is terrifying.

He flips the blade around, wrapping one hand around the flat edge while the other grips my cheeks, squeezing them until my mouth falls open. With a sudden urgency, he kisses me, but before the moment even settles, it's over.

He spits into my mouth, delivers a sharp slap to my cheek, and tugs down his mask. Within seconds, it's all done. I should feel appalled, violated even, but instead, there's a strange liberation in the taste of smoke and peppermint that lingers on my tongue. My gaze fixates on the black mesh holes where his eyes should be, my fingertips brushing against my bottom lip where his mouth should be.

I had only two rules going into this: the mask stays on, and he must never break character. Despite my demands, a desperate curiosity about his appearance gnaws at me. But my wandering thoughts are shattered when he forces the handle into my mouth.

"Get it nice and wet for me, baby."

I suck on the intrusion, coating it with my saliva as he pushes it deeper. I swirl my tongue around the handle, and he slides it in further, then withdraws, fucking my mouth slowly and torturously. He presses it deeper into my throat, until spit gathers and I almost choke. There goes my stellar gag reflex.

The next moment, there's a phone shoved in my face. I really don't want to say the word that's about to come out of my mouth, especially knowing he could have easily stabbed me to death—cunt first. But this is where I draw the line.

"Yellow," I try to say, but my voice is strained and muffled around the knife. I part my fingers in a peace sign and tap them on my arm three times, signaling my safeword.

Wes yanks the knife away, like an intubation tube being forcibly removed from my throat. I suck in a breath as oxygen infiltrates my lungs.

"Yellow," I say again, my voice hoarse.

I rub my throat to ease the pressure and push myself to swallow. Wes tilts his head to the side. "You're going to have to elaborate a little on that one, dead girl. I can't read your mind. Tell me where your head is at." His voice softens, sending a tingle down my spine. But I can't quite tell if he's being sincere or if it's just another part of his game.

"I don't want to be filmed," I rasp. "At least, I don't want to show my face."

As if on cue, my phone vibrates, pulling me from my thoughts.

"You going to get that, dead girl?" he asks, his voice snapping back into a cruel smirk. "It's okay, I'll wait."

I pull the phone from my stocking and swipe up. *Unknown*, again.

I open the message to find a looping video of Wes standing over me, my head tipped back as he pushes the knife handle into my throat. My heart leaps as I realise that someone else, someone I don't know, is filming this. Wes is right here, but the video shows that there's another player in this game. The realisation hits hard: I'm not alone with Wes; someone is watching us. The camera's view is zoomed in on the window from the outside. My

23

heart immediately quickens as I snap my gaze toward the window, but there's nobody there.

Another video pops up, but this time, it's just me, leaning in front of the window, my forearms resting on the windowsill as my head tips back, eyes closed in pleasure, silent cries escaping my parted mouth.

> *Unknown: Does it make your pussy wet knowing you're being watched, dead girl?*

Weirdly, it does. But that doesn't stop the sinking feeling tearing through my gut as I rise from the ottoman, scrambling to face Wes. "Someone's watching us," I say, shoving my phone in his masked face. What if the person in this room with me isn't really Wes?

As I'm bracing myself for him to call off our playtime, he snatches the device from my hands and pockets it. Then he presses the tip of the knife into my chin, tilting it to meet those black holes. "Good little victims don't get to choose how they die, dead girl. So let them watch."

All I need is confirmation that this is part of some delicious plan he's orchestrated. And now I have it. If this other person were a real threat, Wes would undoubtedly reveal his true self.

My gaze follows the tip of the knife as he glides it over my throat, down my neck and chest, until it reaches the edge of my corset.

"Hold still, or I'll cut you," he spits. "But I bet you'd like that, wouldn't you?" Wes pulls the ribbon at the top of my corset. "I could gut you like a fish and your pussy would still weep for me."

What is it about me that makes me instantly soaked at the thought of being helpless and bleeding, begging for mercy as I surrender to his every command?

He hooks the knife underneath the ribbon and pulls it taut, keeping me anchored. In one quick motion, the knife slices through the lacing, exposing the swell of my chest. My nipples, hard and heavy, threaten to tear through the fabric.

"Such a pretty little whore," he coos, his voice dripping with sadistic cruelty, before he raises my phone, filming me. "Such a perfect body in such a silly costume. Are you so desperate for attention that you have to dress like a slut and meet strangers on the internet? Hm? You don't have to dress up on my account, baby, you've already caught my attention." He slices more of the ribbon, tugging my corset strings apart to expose my flesh. "What I really need is to see you beg for your life."

I gaze into the black holes of Wes's mask, biting my lip. "Please don't kill me," I say, looking through my lashes like a good little victim, feigning fear and innocence at his impossibly tall, broad stature. "I'll do anything. Please."

"Killing you would be a damn waste of that body, slut." He hooks two fingers into my mouth and pulls me closer, the musky, slightly sweet taste of leather seeping onto my tongue. "Then again, I'd still fuck this pretty mouth if you were dead. Imagine if you took your last breath on my cock. You've got me so hard thinking about how I could end your life with you choking down my dick," he growls. It's messed up, but it's probably the hottest thing anyone has ever said to me.

May as well book my ticket to hell.

In one swift motion, Wes's knife slices through the remaining lacing. The corset falls to the floor, leaving me exposed in nothing but my tiny skirt and stockings.

"Mm. Perfect," he croons, dragging the tip of the knife from the swell of my chest down to my nipple, pressing the blade into the centre of the puckered bud before retreating to the bed, perching on the edge.

A flash of movement in my periphery catches my attention. Outside, amidst the stillness, a masked figure stands in wait. Instinctively, my hand shoots across my chest, covering my modesty. They're looking straight at me through the window, and it takes everything not to convince myself that this isn't the same person in the hallway or the one on the stairs. Whoever they are, they have the same black hoodie, the same weathered mask, down to the black leather gloves that Wes is wearing.

It's unsettling, yet the thrill of someone watching turns me on more than I care to admit.

"Eyes on me, dead girl," Wes clips. Reluctantly, I turn to face him, trying my hardest to redirect my focus. "Get over here. I want to see you crawl."

Heart racing, I take a breath, too freaked out to return my gaze to the window, but too curious to ignore it. Wes knows fear turns me on, he knows my preferences, my hard and soft limits, and I've mentioned that I'm open to being shared.

I'm perfectly safe.

Steeling myself, I look again, but there's nobody there. Now, I'm left wondering if I'm hallucinating, or if Wes is just that good at messing with me.

4

"Get over here," Wes repeats, his tone commanding. "Crawl to me, dead girl."

I drop to all fours and crawl across the cold surface toward him. As I make my way up his legs, I lay my palms against his shins and rise to my knees. My fingers swiftly work on his buckle. He stands, adjusting his jeans just enough to free his cock from his black briefs.

Fuck. Is there anything about this man that isn't perfect?

I bite my lip, savouring the sight of his swollen head, his shaft adorned with thick, bluish-green veins, and the drop of pre-cum glistening on the tip, begging to be licked.

Bold, colourful tattoos cover the tops of his thick, muscular thighs, extending down to where they hide beneath the black denim. Dragging my nails lightly across the ink, I lick my lips and waste no time wrapping my mouth around him, drawing a groan from him.

My hands press into his thighs as I suck the tip with fervour, flicking the head with my tongue. Then I take him deeper into my mouth, zoning into his noises and the way his chest rises and falls for pacing cues. He tastes like dick should taste, like sweat and skin, and a distinct muskiness that has me salivating. It gets me instantly wet. Sliding my tongue around his shaft, I moan as he eases into my mouth inch by inch.

"Mm, your mouth feels like fucking heaven," he says as I experimentally work my mouth around him, sliding my tongue along the underside of his shaft. I slowly take him to the back of my throat, pulling back repeatedly, building momentum before popping off, a trail of saliva connecting my mouth to his cock.

I spit again, deliberate and rough, as I fist his length, stroking him with my hand while I suck on his tight balls, circling them with my tongue.

"Fuck, Tatum," he hisses. "Such a good little slut for me."

My stomach somersaults as warmth gathers between my legs, his praise driving me to give him the best head of his life. My only goal right now is to make him feel incredible.

He pulls out my phone again. I freeze, popping off while keeping one hand wrapped around his length and the other on his thigh. "Let's make a movie, dead girl. Be my star," he says, his voice low and compelling. "I won't show your face," he reassures me as his finger swipes the screen. "Don't worry, baby. I promise I won't."

I'm not entirely sure how he'll keep my face out of the shot, but his offer is so enticing that I find it hard to refuse. I nod quietly, accepting his request, and dip my head between his thighs. I flick my tongue over his slit, savouring the beads of pre-cum, before sliding him deeper into my throat.

"Fuck, Tatum," he hisses. "Your mouth looks so pretty wrapped around my cock."

The noises this man makes should be illegal. Throaty, guttural, and saturated with so much lust that all my focus is on bobbing my head up and down his dick, wringing out those sounds again and again until he's dripping down my chin.

I'm too focused on Wes that I fail to notice the hands threading through my hair, gripping the base of my scalp, and guiding it onto Wes's wet dick.

I freeze, my mouth still full as their presence sends chills across my spine. I'm too afraid to look, yet too proud and inquisitive not to.

"Keep going, baby. Keep sucking," Wes affirms, his voice strained. "He won't touch unless you ask. Call red if you need to."

Though I have a pretty good idea who's standing behind me, I trust Wes's judgement. Still, I'm wary. Despite my desire to be shared, I dial back my enthusiasm on his dick. What was meant to be exceptional head is slowly becoming mediocre at best.

Wes shifts backward, sliding up the bed to meet the headboard, and I scramble up to join him, my mouth aching with emptiness as I position myself between his legs, eagerly taking his cock between my lips.

The mattress sinks behind me, signalling the stranger's presence. Slow, measured breathing fills the air, and a mysterious, heavy scent—a blend of something dark and sweet—makes me tingle with anticipation. Despite the fear heightening my arousal, I'm too scared to turn around.

I clench my thighs, imagining his gaze tracking over my body, drinking in every inch of my skin, lingering on my glistening pussy. I'm aware that I'm fully bare, folded like a lawn chair with Wes's dick in my mouth, my pussy and ass on full display, aching with need. It's almost pathetic that with one passing thought I've switched from being scared to being so turned on that I'm completely open to this stranger doing whatever the heck he wants to me.

As my mind runs away with me, my tongue elicits another needy groan from Wes's beautiful mouth. My mind conjures an image of him, his sharp jaw clenching, then softening to form a perfect O, a hint of mint and smoke on his breath.

Desperate for stimulation, I push my hips back, grinding them against thin air as I moan around Wes's cock.

"Fuck." The word gusts from his mouth as he lifts his hips, fucking my mouth mercilessly, every thrust stealing my breath as I claw my way underneath Wes's hoodie, digging my fingernails into his skin. His thrusts become shallow, legs shaking as he drives into my mouth. The stranger behind me fists my hair, holding my head still as I await my reward.

Hot, thick spurts of cum shoot across my tongue as Wes's warm pleasure floods my senses, driving me wild. I hold him in my mouth, savouring every pulse as he begins to slow, before swallowing every last drop of his seed.

Wes falls back onto the bed. The stranger's touch softens, their gentle strokes caressing my hair before retreating. My first instinct is to escape, but I've come too far to quit now. I need to see how Wes's master plan unfolds, but he's too busy basking in the afterglow to care.

Rude.

I close my eyes and take a cleansing breath, gathering my composure. With a steady resolve, I turn around to confront a mirror image of the man I've just given my mouth to, complete with mask, black jeans, boots, and gloves—only this one is shirtless.

And he's beautiful.

Colourful tattoos span the entirety of his body, from his well-defined torso to his lean, muscular arms. Thick veins thread the ink, the colours melding together as they creep up and disappear into the black fabric of the mask covering his face. He's slightly shorter than Wes, yet he still towers me. And if the tent in his jeans is any indication, it's that his slim frame doesn't match up to the monster in them.

The entire time he's been here, he hasn't said a word. I don't even know what he looks like, yet I'm so freaking horny at the prospect of two of them succumbing to my every desire that all I can think about is what his dick tastes like.

I look up, my eyes meeting those black holes that I've become accustomed to, wishing I had X-ray vision to watch his expression as my fingertips glide across my tight nipples.

"Are you going to tell me who you are before I suck your cock?" I say, feigning innocence.

But he doesn't move. Doesn't say anything. He just stares at me, feeding my unease.

"Trick won't answer. He's non-verbal," Wes chimes from behind.

A man who doesn't speak? Sounds promising.

"Okay, so how does this work?" I ask, staring at the mask as if willing him to respond. "How are we supposed to communicate?"

"He knows your safeword," Wes says. "He knows everything I know about you." He pauses. "You can bow out anytime. Whatever you need."

It feels intrusive and unfair that this stranger knows my deepest, darkest desires, yet I can't stop staring at the tent in his jeans like it's a wild animal in captivity. And all I want is to set it free.

"No. I don't need my safeword," I say, climbing to the edge of the bed to kneel in front of him while he stands there waiting to get his dick wet. "I want to play." I palm his arousal and glance up at him through my lashes. "Use me, *Trick*."

I take his silence as acquiescence and unzip him, his chest expanding, rising, and falling as I tug down his jeans, then his briefs, his cock springing free mere inches from my mouth. Such a pretty beast.

More colorful ink covers his muscular thighs, descending past his knees and shins; he's a fucking work of art. I dip my head and lick the teardrop muscle above his knee. He shudders, his dick twitching in response. I drag my fingernails across the intricate ink, then wrap my hand around his length.

"Give him your mouth, Tatum. Make him feel good," Wes says, palming my hair.

I stick out my tongue, on my knees like I'm waiting to receive holy communion, closing the distance between my mouth and Trick's cock, and lick the bead of pre-cum leaking from his slit.

"Good girl," Wes says. Trick grips his shaft, tapping the tip onto my tongue before pressing into my mouth. "Our needy little slut."

I take teasing steps to accommodate Trick's impressive cock, stroking him with my tongue as he eases himself in, inch by inch. Sweat, skin, and a distinct sweetness mixed with his unique musk coat my tongue, making me ache between my legs. I grip his shaft and take his length deeper into my mouth.

I can't believe I'm doing this—giving head to a total stranger while another one watches. These guys could be actual serial killers for all I know, but lust knows no boundaries. I'd be doing myself a disservice if I didn't fully embrace this experience.

Wes drags a finger along my slit, making my breath hitch and my pussy ache. "Mm, so fucking wet," he says. I shudder, arching my back, wanting more, while Trick's thick cock repeatedly hits the back of my throat.

A moment later, Wes joins Trick. My eyes instantly land on the thick, hard muscle of his inked torso, to the sheen of sweat glistening in the dip between his pecs, and I follow the trail down his navel to his swollen cock.

I pop off momentarily to marvel at the absolute fucking gods in front of me before Trick presses into me again. If my mouth wasn't already open, it would be gaping at the sight of Wes's shirtless physique.

Never in all my life have I come across a man who could reach full mast ten minutes post-orgasm. Wes is the fucking unicorn I didn't know I needed.

Spit pools at the back of my throat as I suck harder, savouring Trick's taste as he drives into me with reckless abandon, ruthless and wild.

"Do you like how his cock tastes, baby? Does he taste as good as I do?" Wes's words are playful, lacking any trace of jealousy. He's clearly enjoying himself—and so am I.

I am *such* a good little slut.

An incoherent sound brushes past the obstruction in my mouth, affirming Wes's question. He fists my hair, guiding my head as Trick's thrusts intensify, punching air from my lungs and hitting a spot in my throat that triggers my gag reflex.

"I love the way you choke," Wes growls, absently stroking his cock. "Keep going, Tatum. You're being such a good girl for us."

If I could smile smugly, I would. It's almost surreal, having these two all to myself—like I've hit the pinnacle of sluthood, and I'm absolutely revelling in it.

Trick withdraws. My jaw goes slack, aching from the loss, before he plunges his cock back into my throat. He doesn't hold back, but I'm too mesmerised by him to care. The tension in his chest, the divots and the flexion in his lean muscles as he jerks into me, unapologetic and reckless, fucking every coherent thought from my mind. I want to lick every inch of his muscle until he's clawing at me, making me bleed as he silently begs to wreck me.

Wes wraps a hand around my throat, tightening his grip. The force of his fingers makes my eyes want to close, a heaviness settling in my body. Just as I start to drift, he eases up and releases his hold, pulling me back from the edge.

Trick withdraws indefinitely as Wes shoves something wet in my mouth, and it takes me a moment to realise it's my underwear. Except, it isn't my arousal on the fabric.

I fight to resist swallowing the liquid down, but with all the saliva accumulated in my mouth, mixed with this new and unfamiliar, slightly sweet liquid, I squeeze it out.

"Hold it in your mouth, baby. Get a taste for it." Wes's fingers close around my throat, while his other hand grips my cheeks, pressing them to encourage me to swallow.

This is the most reckless thing I've ever done, the most dangerous game I've ever played, and with two complete strangers, nonetheless.

"Do you need to tap out?"

So many thoughts run through my head, but I can only focus on one.

I want this.

"No," I slur, sticky liquid dripping down my chin as I fight to keep my eyes open.

I swear I can almost feel the smile in his voice, sensing their relief. He squeezes my artery, the crushing pressure from his fingertips making my head go light, a weight building behind my eyes.

My pussy clenches, arousal dripping down my thighs as my lungs struggle for air. My eyes flutter open and closed, just enough to make out the two identical, blurry masked figures staring down at me, as if I'm something fucking special. But I'm not, and they'll figure that out soon enough. The thought lingers until it doesn't.

Until it all goes black.

5

I wake up disoriented, my head fuzzy. As my surroundings come into focus, I realise where I am, what I've done, and every event leading up to this.

I let them *drug* me.

But I'm warm.

I'm comfortable.

I'm alive.

And I'm… naked.

Why am I naked?

I scan the room for my clothes, but instead, I see two identical shadows looming at the foot of the bed. Their masked faces are fixed on me, as if they've been waiting for me to wake up—just standing there, silently observing.

"Welcome back, dead girl," Wes says, his voice dripping with mirth, as if I can sense the smirk behind his mask. "How's it feel to be back in the land of the living?"

He circles one side of the bed while Trick moves around the other, handing me a glass of clear liquid. I take it hesitantly, eyeing the swirling contents.

"Relax, it's just water," Wes adds, his tone still laced with that mocking edge.

I sip it, relieved when it actually tastes like water. Each swallow scratches my throat, but it's a small comfort against the dryness.

"You looked so pretty passed out. So peaceful," Wes says, his fingers gently stroking my hair.

"What happened?" I ask, struggling to piece together foggy memories, aware that whatever they drugged me with is still lingering.

"All in due time," Wes replies with a casual shrug.

I turn to Trick. "You've done this before." It's not a question—more of a statement.

"Only when it's strictly consensual," Wes chimes in, answering for Trick.

And there's my answer.

It's ridiculous, but I can't ignore the gut-clenching pang of jealousy that hits me. Ridiculous, because I've known them for barely a few minutes. Of course they've done this before—I only need to look at how well-rehearsed they are to know that.

I should've seen this coming. I always get too attached and fall way too fast. Maybe it's because, despite all the messed-up stuff that's happened, I actually feel kind of safe. Or maybe it's just the drugs they've pumped into me.

Frustrated, I try to get up, pushing through the pain in my hip. As I clamber onto the bed like a newborn deer, I collapse almost immediately.

"Easy," Wes says, grabbing hold of my arm. I ignore him and scramble to kneel on the bed. "Tatum? Slow down. The drugs need time to wear off."

This was supposed to be fun, and I honestly don't know why I'm suddenly throwing a weird, jealous tantrum.

Well, that's the second rule broken.

"I'm fine, I just... I feel like shit," I slur.

My head spins. My body shakes, brimming with nausea. I close my eyes to stem the feeling.

"Shit," Wes says. "It was never meant to make you feel like that." He grips my chin with a gloved hand, forcing my gaze to the blurry black holes of his mask. "We just wanted you to feel good, baby. We can stop this right now. Just say the word. I promise we'll stop if you need us to."

Ugh, why does he have to be so *nice*? It's probably the nausea making me feel icky, but why does he have to focus on my needs and feelings? Whatever was in that magic drug has triggered some strange sensations, conjuring up emotions that I usually keep buried. Hell, if my therapist can't even dig that deep, there's no hope for anyone else. I can't afford to catch feelings for someone who hasn't even made me come yet.

"No." I shake myself from his hold, but all I can do is flop back down onto the pillow. "I want..." My vision blackens. "Let's just..." My limbs feel heavy as I slip away, again.

I want this.

6

I gasp for breath, sharp and violent as I jolt awake, my body lurching forward. The sheets cling to my sweaty skin, binding me to the bed.

"Hello, Tatum," Wes says, tilting his head to the side in true slasher-movie fashion. "Sleep well?"

For a moment, I wonder if the softer Wes I saw before was just a dream. This time, I'm more alert, hyper-aware of everything. Have they pumped me full of something else—adrenaline, maybe? Whatever it is, the gentle side of Wes is nowhere to be found.

I sit upright, clutching the sheets close, a mix of fear and excitement coursing through me as I pull my knees to my chest. Wes stands at the foot of the bed, while Trick is beside me, both shirtless, wearing only their masks and black briefs.

My gaze flickers between them. Trick tilts his head, casually twirling a knife between his fingers. My eyes catch on an empty, discarded needle on the nightstand, leading me to suspect that I've been drugged with something stronger than whatever liquid was soaking my underwear.

Curiosity drives me to slide a hand between my legs, and finding that I'm still intact, I conclude they haven't touched me while I was out cold. So why the drugs?

Trick's stare is calculated. Unnerving. Though the mask hides his face entirely, the weight of his gaze is palpable, pressing down on me like a physical force. He barely moves, yet he exudes a quiet confidence that intrigues me. Despite my vulnerability from my lack of clothing, my body is thriving from the danger, my nipples puckered as they brush the cotton.

"Do you want him baby?" Wes asks, as though he can sense my lust. I nod, forcing my gaze to the black holes of Trick's eyes, licking my lips when it travels down his torso, to the arousal tenting his black briefs. "Don't be shy, dead girl. Tell him what you want."

I rise to my knees, blood rushing to my head and making me dizzy. Kneeling on the edge of the bed, I peel the sheets away, letting them pool around my hips. Every part of me aches with a need to be touched, no—consumed.

"Touch me, Trick. Make me feel good," I plead, dragging my fingernails down his colourful torso.

He reaches out, gripping me by the throat. I hiss, my neck tender from the earlier pressure, but the pain is the sweet torture I crave.

The air between us crackles with tension as his fingers trace slow circles into my skin, kneading away the soreness with deliberate care. Each touch sends electric jolts through my body, amplifying the ache between my legs. Desire pulses from him, a silent force that speaks louder than any words as he strokes me, drawing out my need with every careful motion.

He presses the tip of the knife to my throat, the cold metal biting into my skin as he drags it slowly down my chest, my navel, my pussy…

The cold, hard steel of the blade pressed flat against my clit makes my breath hitch, the stimulation sending a shudder through my body that awakens every nerve.

"Such a good, obedient little slut," Wes says. "Is this what you want? To be used and fucked by two men at the same time? To be worshipped by us? To be completely at our mercy?"

Before I have a chance to answer, Trick pulls the knife away and sets it on the nightstand. Squeezing my throat, he throws me backwards until I'm forced onto my ass, pinned against the headboard.

Wes climbs over me, caging me in. I squirm beneath his solid body, the fear and friction making my pussy clench and my nipples ache.

"Do you want him to play with your pussy while I fuck you?" he growls, his hot, minty breath seeping through the rubber of the mask. When I nod, he presses, "Words, baby. Use those pretty words."

My eyes flick between the two masks before settling on Trick's. "Touch my pussy," I breathe. "Use me."

Trick loosens his hold, his fingertips gently splaying across my neck before trailing down my throat. He pauses to brush my hair over my shoulder, while Wes runs a gloved hand across my nipples. "These tits are so fucking perfect," he says, before giving them a quick little slap. I gasp, embracing the sting as wetness pools between my legs.

Wes lifts his mask just enough to expose his full, pink lips. Without hesitation, he draws my nipple between his teeth, the swirl of his warm tongue sending a sharp rush of electricity through me, making my breath catch.

I gasp as he swiftly moves to the other side, his touch growing more insistent. Each flick of his tongue sends waves of pleasure and urgency through me, making my pulse race.

Kneeling over me, Wes retreats, peeling the remaining sheet down my skin, exposing inch after inch of naked flesh, clammy and prickled with goosebumps as he descends my body. Trick's fingertips follow the path the sheets have left behind, exploring each newly exposed curve. His hand dips between my legs, eliciting a whimper.

"Such a pretty piece of flesh," Wes murmurs as he kneels by the edge of the bed, spreading my knees apart. He produces my phone once again. "You need to see how perfect you are."

He angles the camera towards me, panning it over my body, while Trick's fingers trail over my stomach. Everything feels sharp and new, my consciousness reaching new heights, my awareness fine-tuned to every sensation running through my body.

"Be a good girl and crawl to me, baby."

I crawl to the edge of the bed, tucking my legs beneath me. Wes kneels before me, while Trick resumes his position beside me. I crane my neck to face Trick as his hands roam my body—palms splayed across my stomach and breasts, the leather soft and warm on my nipples as he tugs them between his fingers, then slides his hand back up to wrap around my throat.

His fingers trace my bottom lip before sliding inside my mouth, hooking me behind my bottom teeth. I run my tongue along the backs of his fingers and bite down softly, intoxicated by the addictive, hypnotic energy he radiates. I'm completely captivated. I want to kiss his mask, but more than that, I want to kiss the man behind it.

As I reach for it, he flinches and pulls back. Perhaps he's not ready to reveal himself. Yet, despite the rules I've set for myself, I find the boundaries blurring, my desire pushing me to break them.

If he won't show his face, the least I can do is make sure his cock makes an appearance.

Reaching behind, I palm him through his briefs, eliciting an unexpected, muffled growl that sends a wave of need through my pussy and drives me to continue my pursuit.

There's something almost innocent about stroking a guy through his underwear; it makes me feel virginal and pure, as if I'm rediscovering the thrill of exploring a male body. The thought of him coming this way drives me wild, and I'm tempted to see just how far I can take it. But my thoughts scatter when he removes his fingers from my mouth and presses them between my legs, making me moan through gritted teeth.

Trick prises my legs apart, cupping me, before his finger slides along my slit, making me gasp as I grind my hips against his hand. The feel of his fingers on me is so intense that delaying my release isn't a luxury I have.

Wes kneels beside me, trapping me between him and Trick. His fingers tangle in my hair, yanking my head back so I'm forced to stare at the ceiling. His mouth claims mine with an urgent, almost ruthless intensity. Sweet and torturous, his tongue moves against mine with a practiced precision, as if we've done this countless times before. It's the ultimate mindfuck. Breathless and speechless, I'm left reeling. If this is how he kisses, I can only imagine the way he fucks.

I reach around to cup the back of his head, my fingers slipping under the mask to tangle in his soft, sweat-slicked hair while he palms my breasts. I pull him closer, gripping his scalp to deepen the kiss, moaning into his mouth as Trick drags my nipple through his teeth.

Holy fuck. I think I died and went straight to the depraved depths of hell.

Heat blazes through my body as I grind my hips against the mattress, desperately trying to relieve the burning ache in my pussy. But the pressure is relentless, and it's not enough. I need more.

Trick lowers his mouth to my stomach while Wes moves to my neck, his teeth nipping and biting the sensitive skin. Their synchronised actions intensify the ache between my legs and the marks around my throat. As Wes grips my hips, Trick's face draws closer, just inches from mine.

I lean in, locking my gaze on those depthless black eyes, anticipating a kiss. Instead, he pacifies me by pressing four fingers knuckle-deep into my mouth. Eagerly, I suck on them, moaning as I swirl my tongue around each one, before he withdraws them and shoves them between my legs.

I grind my hips against his hand, watching him intently as he fucks me with his fingers before dragging my nipple into his mouth. Wes covers the areas Trick doesn't, roaming over my breasts and stomach, nipping and biting every inch of exposed skin. His expert tongue swipes along my flesh, and his hands eventually climb up to wrap around my throat.

"You're such a good girl for us, aren't you, baby? Our perfect little slut," Wes murmurs.

His words of affirmation push me closer to the edge, and I can't respond. Instead, I stare into those emotionless black holes that have no right to make me feel this way, especially when I'm so close to release.

The pleasure is overwhelming, leaving me torn between holding back or letting my orgasm consume me. I want to stretch this feeling out, to make it last all night until I'm a sobbing, shaking mess, my body drenched in sweat and sex—filled up, cumdrunk, and utterly satisfied.

The thought makes me rock my hips harder against Trick's hand, my throat making incoherent sounds as Wes repeats his tender praise.

"Do you like that, pretty girl? Does he make you feel good?"

Trick thrusts harder, curling his fingers to hit a sweet spot that has me whimpering, drawing desperate cries from my throat. My walls tighten, my body tense as he brings me to the edge. Just a few more thrusts...

Abruptly, he withdraws his fingers, dragging my nipple through his teeth and cutting off all stimulation. Wes quickly follows suit. My pussy throbs from the sudden emptiness, a deep, unsettling longing that magnifies all my insecurities.

But before I can fully process the sudden shift, Wes grabs my ankles from behind and flips my legs out from under me, eliciting a high-pitched shriek. I land flat on my back, pressed against the mattress with my legs dangling over the edge of the bed. He secures me in a headlock, his knees on either side of my face, his swollen cock conveniently positioned directly above me. Though their faces are hidden, I can sense their amusement from the way they hold themselves.

"Think you're funny, do you? Violating me like this?"

"Yes," Wes quips, dipping his head to give me a chaste kiss before whispering, "we're going to violate you so. Fucking. Hard. And you're going to love every second of it."

His words make my stomach clench and my heart skip a beat. Before I can fully process them, Trick's tongue snaps me back to reality, his relentless invasion of my pussy tearing a cry from my throat.

Pushing my knees to my chest, Trick furiously laps at my cunt, probing me with his tongue, savouring me like he's on death row and I'm his last fucking meal. I reach behind my head and rub Wes's cock through his briefs. He pulls it free and guides it into my mouth, the weight pressing deep into the back of my throat, while he massages my tits.

"Your mouth feels fucking amazing," Wes growls, his hand tightening around my throat as his thrusts become quick and shallow. Trick bites at my pussy, nipping at the flesh of my clit before spitting on it, coating it as his fingers and mouth work in ruthless harmony. "Fuck, Tatum. You look so pretty when you suck my cock."

He jerks his hips, driving his cock deeper, and I choke around him as thick, hot spurts of cum coat my tongue. "Hold it in your mouth, baby."

I do as he says, struggling to breathe while Trick continues his relentless assault on my pussy.

Wes's seed leaks from the corners of my mouth, the sheer degradation amplifying my arousal as I near my limit. "Do you want to come?" he asks.

I nod eagerly.

Wes grips my throat, his fingers tightening just enough to heighten the sensation of my impending orgasm. Trick's tongue curls inside me, hitting that sweet spot again and again, fucking me into oblivion with hard, fast thrusts that draw out waves of intense pleasure.

I moan around the invasion in my mouth, as white spots ghost my vision, and my head goes light.

"Good fucking girl." Wes grips my throat, withdrawing his cock and giving my cheek a sharp smack before kissing me, his cum dripping from my mouth and into my hair. "You're doing so well, baby. Now, swallow for me." I'm quick to comply, swallowing the rest of his seed, savouring the taste. "I love how good you are for us."

The next string of praise, coupled with Trick's sinful tongue, makes my legs shake uncontrollably, my body convulsing as a string of incoherent whimpers pour from my throat. When I come, it's hard and violent. But Trick doesn't let up. Instead, he closes his mouth on my clit and sucks again, pulling another orgasm from me instantly.

"You're so pretty when you come, baby," Wes says. "Do you want to taste yourself?"

I nod. Trick climbs over me, his palms pressing down on either side, pinning me in place. I can barely breathe, my heart racing as he cages me in and finally claims my mouth.

He tastes like me, mixed with mint and smoke and spit. His kiss is soft and teasing, warm like whisky, smooth as honey, and he takes his time, savouring me. I sink into it, completely enveloped by the languid, indulgent quality of his touch—he's exactly what I'm craving.

I tremble as he reaches between my legs, coating his fingers with my arousal before sliding them into my mouth. Our tongues swirl around his fingers, and I savour the addictive blend—a heady cocktail of smoke and musk that leaves me craving more.

Wes tilts my chin towards him and captures my mouth with a fierce, demanding kiss, his intensity a stark contrast to Trick's gentle softness. He pulls back, playfully tugging at my bottom lip with his teeth, leaving me aching for more.

"Ride him, baby," he says. "I want to see you come all over his dick."

My body responds instinctively to his command. I shift into position, breathless with anticipation.

Wes's voice is low and teasing. "Are you ready?"

"Yes," I manage to reply, excitement coursing through me.

I'm on my knees, quite literally, for these men.

7

Wes kneels in front of me, cradling my face as he kisses me, his lips soft and sure. Behind me, Trick moves in sync, holding me tight against him. His mouth skims my neck, hands squeezing my breasts, fingers working their magic between my legs.

I arch my back, pressing my ass against his hardness, rolling my hips with desperate need.

Wes pulls back slightly, his eyes dark with desire. "You look so pretty when you grind against his hand," he murmurs. His mouth descends to my nipple, teeth grazing as his fingers spread possessively across my throat.

In a fluid motion, Wes withdraws, giving Trick space to move. He hooks his hands beneath my legs, an arm sliding across my chest as he flips me effortlessly onto my back. He climbs over me, his weight pressing me into the mattress like a heavy, grounding force.

My breath catches as he plunges two fingers inside me, then withdraws to spread my arousal over my clit. I arch off the bed, hips rising, desperate to meet his mouth. He groans against my lips, the anticipation twisting my stomach in knots, teasing me with the promise of a kiss, that sweet torture of something just out of reach. But he doesn't kiss me. Instead, he pulls the mask back down, and it takes every ounce of restraint not to tear it off his damn face. How fucking dare he?

I don't even care that we can't speak; his actions ignite something raw and primal in me. I'm pissed off, turned on, and craving release.

I hook my legs around his waist, my body begging for his worst, craving as much pain as I can take, both physically and mentally. Perhaps it's because he's a total stranger, and I know I'll never see him—or either of them—again, that I feel so liberated. So fearless.

"Please," I whimper as Trick curls his finger inside my cunt, hitting that sweet spot.

"Please what?" Wes chuckles, his low, sadistic tone only intensifying the ache between my legs. Standing at the foot of the bed, he holds the phone, capturing every desperate plea.

"Hurt me," I plead, clawing at Trick's shoulders, my voice trembling with need. "Fuck me. I want both of you inside me."

Wes smirks, leaning in so his voice sends shivers down my spine. "Beg for it, pretty girl. Tell him exactly what you want."

I grind my hips against Trick's rock-hard cock, digging my heels into his back. "I want it rough. Hard. Make me bleed, make me scream."

Wes's aura darkens, a palpable shift in the air as his voice lowers to a dangerous whisper. "How much does my dirty little slut want another man's cock inside her sweet, tight cunt?"

"I want it more than anything," I gasp, my voice cracking with desperation.

"Beg harder, slut. Prove how much you want it."

"I need you to fill me up, to fuck me so hard I can't think. Please, I'm begging you. I'll do anything. Just give me what I need. I'll be your good little slut—just make me feel it."

Both men exchange a silent look before Trick slides an arm behind my back. In one swift move, he flips us over, leaving me sprawled on top of him, our bodies flush against each other. The brush of my nipples against his chest sends a jolt of electricity straight to my pussy. I press my palms against his chest, pushing myself upright to straddle him, trapping him beneath me with my knees.

Kissing the dip between his pecs, I drag my fingernails over the thick, hard muscle of his chest. His breath hitches as I explore his nipples, circling the metal bars with my tongue and revelling in the way they respond just like mine when I'm turned on—bunched up, tight, and hard. I flick my tongue over the bud, dragging the metal between my teeth, biting the surrounding skin, pulling and sucking until it forms a glistening peak. His breaths become shallow, and he whines, actually whines, and I swear I'm going to explode from that sound alone.

Without wasting another second, I yank down his briefs, freeing his thick, hard cock. It bobs in front of me, and I can't help but marvel at his size, his shape, and the blue-green veins that run along his thick shaft.

I lick my lips, tempted to taste him again, but the need to be filled overwhelms every other thought. I spit on his cock, lift my hips, and align my entrance with the tip. Slowly, I lower myself onto him, savouring the delicious stretch.

"Yes, baby, just like that. Get that tight little cunt nice and stretched," Wes growls from behind us, his voice dripping with lust. "How does he feel?"

"So fucking good," I breathe, taking my time to adjust to his size before fully sinking down, grinding my clit against the dark hair at the base of his shaft. "Oh, my god."

Wes climbs onto the bed behind me, the mattress dipping under his weight. I glance back and see him fisting his cock in one hand while holding my phone in the other. He sets the phone down briefly, freeing his hand to grab the back of my neck. Then he pushes me down, pressing my body flush against

Trick's. The slickness of my arousal and spit coats my clit as I grind against Trick's pelvis.

"Please," I whimper. I don't know what for. Something. *Anything.*

Trick grips my hips, holding me steady as I writhe and ache for more. Just as the edge of my orgasm starts to build, he pulls out, and Wes takes his place with brutal force. His thrusts knock the breath from my lungs as my walls tighten around him. He feels different—perhaps it's the angle or the relentless way he fucks, as if he's determined to leave a mark inside me. What's worse is that I'd welcome internal bruising with open arms... or should that be legs?

Once I get used to the feel of Wes, he withdraws, letting Trick drive into me again. This time, Trick's thrusts match Wes's—brutal, punishing, and bruising, just the way I like it. They take turns, tag-teaming my pussy: Wes behind me, his hands fisting my hair, while I grind my clit against Trick.

"You feel so fucking good, baby," Wes breathes, his words brushing the shell of my ear and sending a shiver of excitement down my spine.

"Fuck... Oh, my god... I'm going to come," I cry.

Stars explode behind my eyes as my body convulses. Every nerve tingles with pleasure, waves of ecstasy crashing over me as another orgasm tears through me, setting my body alight.

I bury my head into Trick's chest, his heartbeat muffling my cries. I lose myself in the afterglow, waiting patiently for the climax to subside and my breath to return to normal.

Wes's voice cuts through the haze, dark with anticipation. "Well done, baby. Ready for more?"

A part of me wants to keep pushing, to embrace the intensity and prove my endurance. But as I try to focus, I realise just how exhausted I am. My pussy is sore, my legs feel like jelly. I want to cry from the sheer effort, but I also want to keep pushing through and do the hot girl shit. "I... I can't. I can't come again."

"That's not your decision to make," Wes says, his tone firm. "You're ours for the night, remember? Free use. Unless you'd rather tap out, we get to have you as we please. Just know that we're not going to stop until we've had our fill."

He's right; free use was part of the agreement. I want them to use me, but physically, I'm drained.

Wes lowers his voice, a note of tenderness softening his intensity. "Don't worry, baby. We'll take care of you. If you need a break, just let us know. We'll make sure you're okay."

Behind me, I feel the warm, wet trail of spit dripping slowly down my slit.

"Deep breaths, baby. We're going to fuck you in this tight little cunt. Together."

Trick enters me again, making me gasp as he buries himself to the hilt, while Wes teases my entrance with his fingers.

"It won't fit," I say through gritted teeth.

"Just relax. We'll make it fit. You were made for us, dead girl," Wes replies, his voice low and confident.

I manage a strained smile, muttering, "I'm glad someone in this room is feeling positive."

A low chuckle escapes his mouth as he scissors two fingers inside me, stretching me slowly as he gradually forces his way in, filling me inch by inch. I feel like I'm being ripped apart, but the pain mingles with an undeniable pleasure. And it hurts so fucking good.

Embracing the burn, I breathe through the discomfort as Wes starts moving inside me. Trick stays still, his breathing in sync with mine. I watch his chest rise and fall while Wes's cock slides against Trick's inside me, sparking a fresh wave of need. It's all I can do not to grind against them.

"That's our good girl. Such a dirty little slut for us," Wes says. The thought of their cocks rubbing together makes me wild with desire.

I focus on the euphoric intensity of his slow, deliberate thrusts as both men fill me completely, Wes's words driving me closer to my release. "Our dirty." *Thrust.* "Little." *Thrust.* "Slut."

He slows and then stops, anchoring his cock inside me, giving Trick the chance to drive into me from below. Trick pounds into me relentlessly, his thrusts deep and brutal, making my body convulse and clench with every motion.

My mind turns to jelly, every coherent thought completely fucked out of it. I'm a mindless, slutty little dead girl getting fucked raw and ragged just like I deserve. God, I hope they leave a mark.

"Don't fight it, baby. Scream baby scream," Wes says, his voice edged with a touch of madness.

On Wes's command, I rub my clit greedily against Trick, grinding my hips into his pelvis. And I scream. I scream until my throat feels raw, until my lungs are starved for air and my breath comes in shallow gasps.

My body is drenched in sweat, muscles tensed as pressure builds in my head.

My orgasm overwhelms me—intense, unstoppable, soul-shattering. Incoherent words tumble from my mouth as they continue their relentless pursuit. I'm lost somewhere between pure euphoria and a surreal, otherworldly state.

Trick shudders beneath me, his orgasm claiming him as I convulse again, another explosive climax tearing through me. Wes thrusts urgently, pushing me higher into this dizzying wave of bliss. I feel like I'm floating between dimensions, completely transcending reality.

Wes groans, his breathing shallow as his cock jerks and convulses while his hands grip my hair. We collapse into a tangled heap, my head nestled into Trick's shoulder while Wes's rests against the back of mine. I'm completely spent, too drained to even lift my head, let alone make a trip to the bathroom. I focus on my breathing, syncing with the rise and fall of their chests.

Wes's lips brush against my neck. "You did so well, baby. We're so proud of you." He rolls to the edge of the bed, giving me enough space to slide between them. I'm left with the choice of staying on top of Trick's warm, solid body or dealing with the cum-soaked sheets. Despite the warmth, I opt for the latter. I've never been one for cuddling, anyway. I roll off Trick and position myself between the two men who have, without a doubt, flipped my world—and all my expectations—upside down.

"You good?" Wes asks, breaking the charged silence.

"Better than good," I reply.

Trick wraps his arm around me as I trace my fingernails along the planes of his stomach. Now that we're satiated, I take a closer look at his tattoos. Angels, cherubs, winged creatures, and mythical beasts in shades of red, white, black, and turquoise hold me captive. His arm furthest from me is completely blacked out with white floral detailing, and I can't help but wonder if it's a cover-up or just a trend thing.

"Who got you smiling like that?" Wes's mask looks almost comical now that I've fulfilled my depraved little fantasy. I didn't even realise he was watching me.

"Who do you think?" I say, the blush creeping on my cheeks having nothing to do with the fact that I'm overheated, overstimulated, and worn out.

"Hey, Tatum. Trick or treat?" Wes's hands slowly slide to the bottom of his mask.

"Don't," I say, surprising myself with the abruptness. He freezes, fingers hooked on the mask's edge. I'm curious to see his face, but I'm not ready to confront the reality of their identities after what we've just done, after feeling so exposed. "Keep it on."

"Playtime's over, princess," Wes says, his voice edged with something I can't quite place without a facial expression.

"I think it's better if I don't know what either of you look like. You know, keep the fantasy alive and all that." I try to sound playful, though I'm struggling to keep my composure as I swallow around the lump in my throat.

How do I tell them I don't want the night to end? That seeing their faces would make this feel too real?

This was supposed to be a fantasy. One night. Then I could be satisfied and move on. But the longer the night goes on, the harder it becomes to accept that this might end.

Wes sighs. "As you wish. But it's coming off the moment you fall asleep."

Fair game.

8

I have a moment of silence for my long-suffering bladder *et al*, as my eyes flicker open. Light filters through the window, casting the room in soft shades of gold. I'm dressed in a pair of men's briefs and a black T-shirt that smells faintly of smoke, sweat, and musk. There's nobody beside me, but a dip in the mattress and a groan signal someone behind me.

I roll off the bed, the ache between my legs catching me off guard as I step onto the cold floor and catch a glimpse of my wild state in the mirror. I look like shit, but I regret nothing.

I take a cleansing breath and sneak a glance behind me, expecting to see the ghost-like mask this early in the morning. Instead, I'm met with a real human face, and I know from his build and tattoos that it's Wes.

Fuck, I'm so screwed.

He's absolutely fucking gorgeous, because why the fuck wouldn't he be?

I should be relieved, but instead, all I feel is existential dread in the pit of my stomach. This shouldn't complicate things, but it does. And the more I gawk at him, the harder it will be to walk away and forget.

Messy, dark hair covers half of his face, stuck to his skin, slick with sweat. Piercings in both nostrils of an aquiline nose, and a hole on one side of his lip where metal should be, stretched ears with small black plugs, and grown-out stubble on a prominent jaw...

And the prettiest brown eyes I've ever seen.

It takes me a moment to realise that I'm staring at him open-mouthed, fangirling over how handsome he is, while I'm over here looking like I've just crawled out of a grave. I must be quite the spectacle to wake up to.

"Good morning, dead girl," he says, his raw morning voice stirring my insides. As if my pussy needs any more attention after last night.

"Hey, I was just—"

"Bailing?"

Uh-oh. Busted. "Um... yeah."

"Last night was fun. I had a really good time," he says.

"Me too." As the silence stretches awkwardly, I scramble for something to say. "So, where did Trick go?"

"You know that's not his real name, right?" His smirk has no right to affect me the way it does.

"You know that didn't answer my question, right?" I counter, raising an eyebrow.

Wes smirks. "Must have had the same idea as you and bailed."

Tou-fucking-*ché.* "Maybe," I reply, shrugging slightly.

What am I waiting for? Goodbyes aren't usually this awkward. Then again, I usually take what I want and leave before they wake up.

I find my boots and perch on the edge of the bed to pull them on. "I guess I'll see you around, then," I say, attempting to sound casual.

"That's it?" Wes asks, his tone tinged with a mix of curiosity and disappointment.

I finish tying my laces and stand up, turning back to face him. "Let's not pretend this is more than what it is. I've spent most of my twenties naive to the realities of hooking up. I know how this works." And I'd be doing myself a disservice if I thought this was anything more. "We all got what we wanted."

"Whatever you say, Tatum." He sits against the headboard and runs a hand through his hair. "Man, Wes is going to be pissed."

"Wes?"

"Trick or treat," he says, flashing a smile that could melt my panties off—if I were wearing any.

A flood of thoughts crashes through my mind. The words of the man I thought was Wes from last night swirl in my head: *"He knows your safeword. He knows everything I know about you."*

The realisation hits me like a blow to the head.

"Wait. Trick is the one I've been talking to this entire time?"

Not-Wes nods, a smirk tugging at his lips. "Surprise, Tatum."

Fuck. I feel like I've just had a rug pulled beneath me. It explains the reason why Not-Wes seemed bigger in real life compared to his photos, and why the photos were always taken in the dark, and why we never spoke on the phone. "He didn't know how you'd feel about him if you knew the truth."

"Because he doesn't speak? Why would that bother me?"

"He said that dirty talk seems to be your thing, given your entire chat history revolves around it. He was worried you might lose interest if he couldn't give you that."

Wow. He orchestrated this entire plan just for me. It's sad to admit, but no one has ever gone above and beyond like this before. Despite feeling a bit duped, I have to admit that—in a world that often feels transactional—I'm genuinely impressed.

"And that's where you come in? Are you... together?"

"He's my best friend. And I suppose I'm kind of a mediator."

"So that's why there was two of you. It all makes sense now." I pause, an uneasy feeling settling in my gut. "You seem to know what you're doing."

"If that's your way of asking if this is a regular thing for us, it isn't. I mean it when I say that last night was special. We both feel that way." He slides off the bed, moving closer to me as he speaks.

"What happened last night? When I was out?" I ask, bracing myself for his answer.

"We didn't fuck you, if that's what you're asking." Relief washes over me, tinged with a strange sense of disappointment. I can't help thinking that if there was ever a next time, I would want them to. He steps closer, standing next to me. I instinctively take a step back, finding myself near the door.

"We gave you a sedative. And we filmed the rest. Everything you need to know is on your phone."

"Thanks."

"You know we wouldn't intentionally hurt you, right?"

I'm starting to. "I know."

"Last night was a test run, baby. I think I can speak for both myself and Wes when I say that we'd like to see you again." His warm, sulphuric breath fans the shell of my ear as he backs me against the door, his raw, natural scent drawing me in. "You were perfect, Tatum," he whispers.

And just like that, he has me soaked between my legs.

Focus, Tatum.

His mouth hovers over my neck for a moment before he pulls back. "Now, go and find your boy."

He steps away, letting me face the door. As I reach for the handle, I pause.

"I'm Ash, by the way," Not-Wes says. I stop, his voice drawing me back. "In case you want to scream my name for real next time."

"I'll keep that in mind," I reply, smiling at the thought of a possible next time, as I leave the room and close the door on another chapter of my messed-up life.

9

It's barely even daylight as I descend the final step into the entryway, where less than twelve hours ago I stood, full of excitement and eager anticipation, oblivious to how the night would unfold. Despite the early hour, everything feels clearer somehow. Every room is empty. There's nobody here. It's almost like the party never happened.

But the stack of pizza boxes covering a portion of the worktop, and a cluster of bin bags by the back door tells me otherwise. On the kitchen island, there's a takeaway coffee cup with my name scrawled across it, a brown paper bag, and... my phone. On the assumption that there's only one person in this house who this was meant for, I open the bag.

The almond croissant has me salivating, just thinking about that sweet, buttery fix I've been craving. I take a big bite, savouring the flaky layers, and pop open the lid of my coffee. As soon as I breathe in the warm, spicy aroma of my pumpkin spice latte, that sugary cinnamon goodness hits me, making this October staple feel like the perfect cosy treat.

I wrap up the croissant and head outside with my breakfast, stepping around a small mountain of bin bags by the back door. I make a mental note to find the wheelie bin and deal with the mess—it's the least I can do after bailing on a party to fuck not one, but two random strangers.

The morning air is eerily quiet, an unsettling kind of calm that makes me wonder where everyone has gone. I sink into the outdoor sofa, eyes drifting across the empty garden as I unlock my phone and open my gallery. The screen fills with videos—clips of me, 'Wes,' and 'Trick,' all so familiar, yet now carrying a different weight. One video, in particular, catches my eye—a shot of me, unconscious on a bed.

I hit play, anticipation mingling with a strange sense of satisfaction. In the video, Wes—his slighter frame unmistakable—moves toward my still body. I watch with rapt attention as he injects a clear liquid into my arm, the syringe vanishing as quickly as it appeared. A slow smile tugs at my lips as he heats the blade of a knife with a lighter, the flickering flame illuminating the dark room. My pulse quickens, not with fear, but with the thrill of seeing him press the glowing blade to my skin, carving into my flesh with deliberate precision.

I continue watching, captivated, as they take turns marking me. Each incision is a claim, a testament to something I can't quite name but know I crave. Wes eventually dresses my wound with practiced care, his touch both tender and possessive, before pulling the sheet over my body. The camera cuts out, leaving me with the image of my seemingly peaceful self, a stark contrast to the excitement thrumming just beneath my skin.

Without hesitation, I lift my T-shirt and peel away the dressing, hissing softly as fresh blood oozes from the wound. The sight is raw, visceral, but it doesn't repel me. It draws me in. The pain is muted, almost an afterthought, drowned out by the satisfaction of knowing those marks are mine. How did I not feel this last night? And why do I barely feel it now? I press my fingers gently against the wound, a shiver of pleasure running through me. The peaceful morning around me feels like a facade, masking the dark, thrilling secret I now carry, etched into my flesh.

Unknown: Enjoying your breakfast?

Startled, I jerk my head up, tugging the T-shirt down and quickly closing the video. The screen goes dark, my reflection staring back at me with wide eyes and a racing heart. Then, something else catches my eye—a shadowy figure, just behind me, mirrored in the black glass.

My breath hitches, heart pounding in my throat. I whip around, but the space behind me is empty, the morning air still and silent. A nervous laugh escapes me, tinged with the edge of doubt. Either I'm losing my mind, or he's really fucking good at lurking in the shadows. The thought sends a shiver down my spine, a mix of fear and excitement twisting in my gut. I can't tell if I want him to be there or if the idea terrifies me more than I'm willing to admit.

Did he just happen to guess that I'm a pumpkin spice fan? That almond croissants are my ultimate comfort food? The thought sends a chill down my spine. Maybe he's been watching me longer than I realised. Or maybe I'm just reading too much into this, clutching at something real so last night doesn't have to end here.

Maybe I shouldn't like that idea so much.

I counter his question with a *you got me* in the hope that I'll finally get to see his face. After all, I was well and truly tricked—it's the least I deserve. What's one more rule being broken at this point?

"Come out, come out, wherever you are," I whisper to myself, a mix of challenge and anticipation lacing my voice. Suddenly, my phone vibrates in my hand, startling me.

Unknown: Tatum.

I watch the bubbles dance across the screen, eagerly awaiting the message.

Unknown: My sweet, haunted house.

My heart pounds with anticipation as I sense his presence before I see him. Finally, the real Wes steps out of the shadows, a dark force dressed in black, his figure imposing and magnetic. The colorful ink on his thigh peeks through the rips in his jeans, vibrant against the monochrome of his outfit. He's impossible to ignore, every inch of him demanding my attention.

I suck in a breath, steeling myself for the moment I've been both dreading and craving. Slowly, I lift my gaze to his. His face is obscured beneath a black hood, but I can just make out a straight nose and a sharp jaw, half-hidden in shadow. The details are teasingly out of reach, keeping him cloaked in mystery.

Before I can fully process the sight of him, he types something on his phone. My gaze drops to my lap as my phone vibrates, the familiar buzz sending a jolt through me. The message is waiting, but I hesitate, caught between the thrill of the unknown and the reality of the man standing just inches away.

Unknown: We may have caught you,
but it doesn't mean we're done
chasing you.

Kneeling before me, Wes pulls off his hood, revealing a mass of unruly black curls that frame his face. As he lifts his gaze to meet mine, the intricate floral ink covering his throat draws my eyes, but it's the intensity of his stare that truly holds me captive.

And I swear my heart stops beating.

Beautiful doesn't even begin to describe him. He's a living masterpiece—a perfect blend of raw strength and delicate artistry. His strong jaw, straight nose, and those eyes—so impossibly blue they're almost blinding, like staring directly into the sun—leave me completely mesmerised. In this moment, our strange, serendipitous connection feels like the only thing that matters.

I must be drooling, because in the next breath, a smile tugs at his lips, revealing a set of straight, white teeth that somehow make him even more devastatingly perfect.

And there it is. That heart-stopping, panty-melting smile is my undoing. It's like he's reached into my chest and taken hold of my heart, leaving me breathless, helpless, and undeniably his.

"You're so..." I begin, but the words tangle in my throat, lost in the whirlwind of emotions flooding my mind. It's hard enough to form a coherent thought, let alone string a sentence together when he's this close, when his presence is so overwhelming.

Wes presses a finger to his beautiful lips, silencing me with a gesture as familiar as it is mesmerising. Just like the first time I saw him on the stairwell at the party, that simple motion leaves me breathless, suspended in the moment. He doesn't say a word, but the command is clear.

Without breaking eye contact, he pulls out his phone, his fingers moving swiftly as he types another message. The anticipation builds as I wait, my heart pounding in sync with the quiet vibration that soon follows.

> *Unknown: Can you be quiet for me, Tatum?*

I nod.

> *Unknown: Good girl. Wouldn't want to wake up your friends.*

Pocketing his phone, Wes sinks to his knees, shifting his attention back to me. His gaze locks onto mine with an intensity that makes my pulse quicken. I try to focus on the house, reminding myself that Cara and Daisy must have crashed here with the other guests, but all thoughts scatter when Wes places his palms on my thighs. With a firm tug, he pulls them apart, his thumbs pressing against my soaked cunt through the damp fabric of my borrowed briefs.

His head dips between my legs, and he plants a slow, deliberate kiss on my pussy, his tongue trailing a line from slit to clit through the cotton. The sensation draws a sharp breath from my lungs, a mix of pleasure and longing. I'm sore, my body aching from the night before, but all I can think about is how much I want him.

"Don't stop," I plead, the words spilling out as he sucks my clit into his mouth, his lips and tongue working in perfect, agonising rhythm. His hands slide underneath my shirt, exploring the familiar terrain of my skin. Suddenly, his thumb twists into my open wound, and I hiss in pain, a new wave of fresh blood trickling from the cut. But he's relentless, the sharp sting only amplifying the pleasure as he continues to suck and lick me through the fabric.

The contrast between the pain and the pleasure, the rough and the tender, leaves me trembling, lost in the overwhelming sensations he's creating. Every touch, every movement, drags me deeper into a place where all I can feel is him.

I come almost instantly, my cries of release escaping long and loud as Wes's tongue and that magical fucking mouth continue to coax every last shudder from me. My body goes limp, sinking back into the sofa, utterly spent. I'm not even sorry for the loss of control. If anything, he should be the one apologising for being such a goddamn enigma. I'm determined to unravel the mystery of Wes, even if it means losing myself in the process.

He retreats, leaving me breathless and dazed. As I lift my T-shirt, I glide my fingertips over my open wound, feeling the blood smear as it leaks from the two identical words carved into my flesh. *Mine.* The writing is unmistakable, each word clearly etched by different hands, shallow yet deep enough to leave a temporary scar. The sight of it sends a shiver down my spine, a mix of discomfort and strange satisfaction.

An urgent curiosity grips me, compelling me to finish watching the footage from last night. I need to know exactly what I missed while I was passed out, to piece together the full story. But as I look at the marks on my skin, I'm haunted by a different question: How will I feel once last night is a distant memory and all that remains are these scars?

My phone vibrates again, jolting me from my tangled thoughts.

Unknown: You're so fucking beautiful when you come.

Heat flushes my cheeks as I watch him type out another message, his expression unyielding and solemn.

Unknown: This doesn't have to be over if you don't want it to be. Just say the word.

He stands, and I follow, refocusing my gaze on his intense blue eyes, which shift between darkness and light, yin and yang.

I give in to the realisation that I'm not ready for this to end. I want more—more of this, more of us. I crave his depravity, his softness, caught between the thrill of being chased and the comfort of being caught.

"Wes?" I say, my voice steady but laden with desire. His gaze darkens further at the sound of his name. "Maybe you could keep me a little longer," I continue, my words laced with a mixture of longing and hope. "Until Halloween is over, at least. Until the scars heal."

A slow, knowing smile curves his lips as he types another message on his phone, the movement deliberate and full of unspoken meaning. The seconds stretch into an agonising wait as the anticipation of his response fills the space between us.

Unknown: I'd like that.

A stray lock of hair falls across his eyes as he types again, the gesture both casual and unexpectedly intimate.

Unknown: And I like hearing you say my name, almost as much as I love hearing you scream.

A smile tugs at the corners of my mouth, my pulse quickening at his words. "I love saying your name," I reply softly, letting the sentiment linger in the air.

Unknown: Well, then, my pretty dead girl. This won't end here.

Epilogue

Wes

The nightclub pulses with electric energy, the bass thumping through my chest as I scan the crowded room. Tatum stands at the bar with her friends, laughing and chatting, her eyes sparkling under the flashing lights. She's completely unassuming, blissfully unaware of our plan. Ash and I have been scheming this for weeks; she just doesn't know it yet.

As I move toward her, I discreetly pull out a small vial of GHB from my pocket. With practiced ease, I pour the contents into her drink, the clear liquid blending seamlessly. I slip away into the crowd, my movements smooth and unnoticed. The drug will dissolve quickly, and within ten minutes, it will begin to take effect—keeping her conscious yet compliant, heightening her pleasure while blurring her awareness.

She takes a sip of her drink, and we linger in the shadows, buzzing with anticipation as we watch the drug take effect. Her laughter starts to drag, her movements getting slower and more fluid. It's working—just like we planned.

My hands are sweaty, and my throat feels like sandpaper, but I'm not about to step out into the open. Staying hidden is way safer; one wrong move and it's game over. My heart's pounding so hard I can practically hear it in my ears, every thump adding to the rush of adrenaline.

When Tatum finally heads to the bathroom, Ash and I lock eyes. This is it—the moment we've been waiting for. My pulse is racing, and I'm practically vibrating with excitement as we slip through the crowd. Every second feels like a lifetime, and I'm revved up, ready for whatever comes next.

We find her alone in the bathroom, and I'm quick to act. I slam my hand over her mouth, using my arm to pin her against the stall as I shove her inside. She squeals and kicks, trying to break free, but I tighten my grip. There's no way I'm letting her slip away.

Ash slips in and locks the door behind him, the click echoing ominously. I turn her around to face us. Her eyes widen with fear but quickly shift to recognition, and then to a glazed, almost dreamy look as the drug kicks in. She sighs, her body going limp against mine. I catch her, my senses flooded by her intoxicating vanilla-cinnamon scent.

Ash's calm presence is a steadying force as we guide her. I lock eyes with Tatum, her gaze now half-closed and unfocused, and I feel a rush of mixed emotions—protectiveness tangled with desire. She's ours now, fully and willingly.

Together, we undress her, carefully supporting her weight as my fingers graze her warm skin, feeling the slight shivers of anticipation running through her. Her breathing is quick and shallow, her body reacting even in this dazed state.

As I pull her skirt up around her waist, my eyes fall on the scars on her side—uneven and marred, as if she's been picking at them, almost like she wanted them to be a permanent part of her. They're healed but far from pristine, a stark reminder of our last encounter. I find myself almost missing the rawness they once held.

Ash steps in front of her, his touch a mix of firmness and tenderness as he holds her steady. "Look at our girl, Wes," he murmurs, his voice thick with lust. "She's so perfect, so trusting."

I nod, my hands exploring her curves, feeling the heat of her body against mine. The small, confined space of the stall intensifies every sensation, every touch, every breath.

Ash sinks to his knees, tugging her thong down to suck on her clit. Tatum sighs, a soft little sound that has my heart racing and my dick threatening to tear a hole in my jeans.

From behind, I glide my finger along her slit, sinking two fingers inside her warm, wet cunt. Soft whimpers escape her throat, igniting a rush of blood straight to my dick.

Ash's fingers meet mine, our movements synchronised, our breaths mingling in the confined space. "Fuck, baby. You're so wet for us," he says, biting his lip, as wetness floods her needy and wanting little cunt.

Tatum's moans are soft, almost inaudible, but I can feel their vibrations through her body as she surrenders to us.

She moves freely within my grasp, lighting up with every thrust of our fingers, every swipe of Ash's tongue, as sweat slicks her pale skin.

I'm so proud of her. Of us. This is the ultimate trust, the ultimate gift she could give us.

I cover her moans with my hand, muffling her cries as she bucks against me, my dick throbbing with every grind of her perfect ass against me. The heat of her breath fogs up my fingers, mingling with the dampness of her skin.

"That's our good girl, Tatum," Ash murmurs. "Come for us, baby."

She collapses into me, her face twisting in ecstasy as her body trembles and convulses in a symphony of pleasure and surrender. Her pussy grips our fingers tightly, the sweet fucking melody of her release echoing in the confined space.

I catch her as she sags, holding her close, anchoring her while my heart pounds with the thrill of almost getting caught. I'd face any consequences to make her depraved fantasies a reality.

As Ash dresses her and whispers affirmations, I brush the damp hair from her face and trace the delicate lines of her features with my fingers, soothing her where words fall short.

So perfect.

Ash leans in, his voice a low, almost seductive whisper in my ear. "We should mark her again, Wes. She belongs to us."

I look down at our pretty girl, her eyes fluttering open, still glazed and dreamy, lost in euphoria. She's practically melting into my embrace, trusting us completely. The idea of marking her again sends a rush of excitement through me. I can't help but get hard just imagining it. It would be so easy to take a knife to her skin right here and now—taking turns with Ash to fuck her and mark her, our cum dripping from her swollen cunt while her skin bears our twisted marks.

But as much as I want to, I can't go that far this time. We've pushed her limits for tonight, and I want to savour the control we have without going overboard. Besides, leaving her with a memory of us, something she'll want to come back for, is far more satisfying.

"Another time," I sign.

We make sure her needs are taken care of, checking her vital signs just to be thorough. Once we're satisfied, we slip away, leaving her in the stall. We melt into the shadows, keeping a close eye on the bathroom door to make sure she's safe.

Eventually, she stumbles out, looking slightly unsteady but otherwise composed, with a sly, satisfied smile on her face as she rejoins her friends. I can't help but notice how she keeps glancing around the room, almost as if she can feel us watching.

Ash and I exchange a satisfied glance. The thrill of the game lingers between us, making our connection even stronger. We've pushed boundaries, tested limits, and turned our darkest cravings into reality.

The future is tangled and uncertain. But as I watch her now, I can't shake the feeling that someday she'll be exactly where we want her—screaming for more.

Acknowledgements

I want to extend a huge thank you to Sandy and Stef for being the best betas a girl could ask for. Your amazing feedback has been invaluable, and I honestly don't know what I'd do without it. To the rest of the pastry gang—Sarah and Skye—thank you for always being there to answer my questions and for your ongoing support. I love you all so much.

A special shoutout to Ria for delivering yet another stunning cover. Your work never fails to impress me, and I'm so grateful for the opportunity to work with you again—long may our projects continue!

TO ZAINAB (ZEE), YOU'RE A LEGEND! THANK YOU FOR TAKING MY ROUGH DRAFT AND WORKING YOUR MAGIC TO POLISH IT INTO SOMETHING TRULY

SONIA PALERMO

SPECIAL. I SERIOUSLY DON'T KNOW WHAT I'D DO WITHOUT YOU!

And to my readers, my family and friends, and everyone who has supported me with this book—ARC readers, Bookstagrammers, BookTokers, and more—THANK YOU! I'm endlessly grateful for your support and encouragement. I hope you love this book!

Last but not least, a nod to Skeet Ulrich and Matthew Lillard for sparking my love of horror and morally complex characters. Here's to many more sexy adventures!

ABOUT THE AUTHOR

Sonia Palermo writes spicy contemporary, paranormal, and erotic romance. When she's not immersed in writing, she enjoys cosying up on the sofa with a cup of tea and indulging in a good horror or romance movie. A true beach lover, Sonia finds inspiration along the beautiful south coast of England, where she lives. The serene seaside surroundings bring a touch of real-life magic to her stories.

Sonia's work reflects her passions—spooky atmospheres, intense romance, and the charm of everyday moments, inviting readers to discover where the ordinary meets the extraordinary, with a happily ever after guaranteed.

ALSO BY SONIA PALERMO

Hot Girl Summer
Papillon

www.ingramcontent.com/pod-product-compliance
Ingram Content Group UK Ltd.
Pitfield, Milton Keynes, MK11 3LW, UK
UKHW010755220925
8009UKWH00040B/335

9 781739 996338